Rola Polar Bear and the Heatwave

Blackie Bears

Rola Polar Bear and the Heatwave

Elisabeth Beresford

Illustrated by Janet Robertson

A Blackie Bear

To Charlie and Ben with love from Granny Liza

BLACKIE CHILDREN'S BOOKS

Published by the Penguin Group
Penguin Books Ltd, 27 Wrights Lane, London W8 5TZ, England
Penguin Books USA Inc., 375 Hudson Street, New York, New York 10014, USA
Penguin Books Australia Ltd, Ringwood, Victoria, Australia
Penguin Books Canada Ltd, 10 Alcorn Avenue, Toronto, Ontario, Canada M4V 3B2
Penguin Books (NZ) Ltd, 182–190 Wairau Road, Auckland 10, New Zealand

Penguin Books Ltd, Registered Offices: Harmondsworth, Middlesex, England

First published 1994
1 3 5 7 9 10 8 6 4 2

Text copyright © Elisabeth Beresford, 1994
Illustrations copyright © Janet Robertson, 1994

The moral right of the author and illustrator has been asserted

Filmset in 15/20pt Linotron Plantin Educational by
Rowland Phototypesetting Ltd, Bury St Edmunds, Suffolk
Printed and bound in Great Britain by
Butler & Tanner Ltd, Frome, Somerset

A CIP catalogue record for this book is available from the British Library

ISBN 0–216–94121–0

About the Author

Elisabeth Beresford is an established children's author. This is her third book for Blackie in the Blackie Bear series, her first two being *Tim the Trumpet* and *Jamie and the Rola Polar Bear*. She has written over one hundred books, including the enormously popular Wombles series. She is a freelance writer and journalist, and has frequently broadcast on television and radio. She has also spent time in Africa, giving talks to children in schools. Although she was born in Paris, Elisabeth now lives on Alderney, in the Channel Islands. In between her writing she even finds time to work as a Station Master on the Alderney Railway!

Jamie stared out of his bedroom
window. He could just see his
mother as a head and shoulders
down on the street. She was on her
way to the supermarket and then to
work.

Jamie gave an enormous sigh,
which was odd because it was
another beautiful hot day. The
trouble was that Jamie knew his
great friend the Rola Polar Bear

only liked cold weather. *Really* cold weather, because his home was at the North Pole. The heat made him scratch so that his fur stood up in tufts. Rola Polar didn't complain – he wasn't the complaining sort – but Jamie could see how uncomfortable he was. Jamie was very worried that one day Rola Polar would say, 'Sorry, but I've just *got* to go home . . .'

Jamie put some cold water in the washing-up bowl and added all the ice cubes he could find in the fridge, just as Rola Polar came down from his shed on the roof of the flats.

'Morning,' he said, coming into the kitchen without Jamie hearing

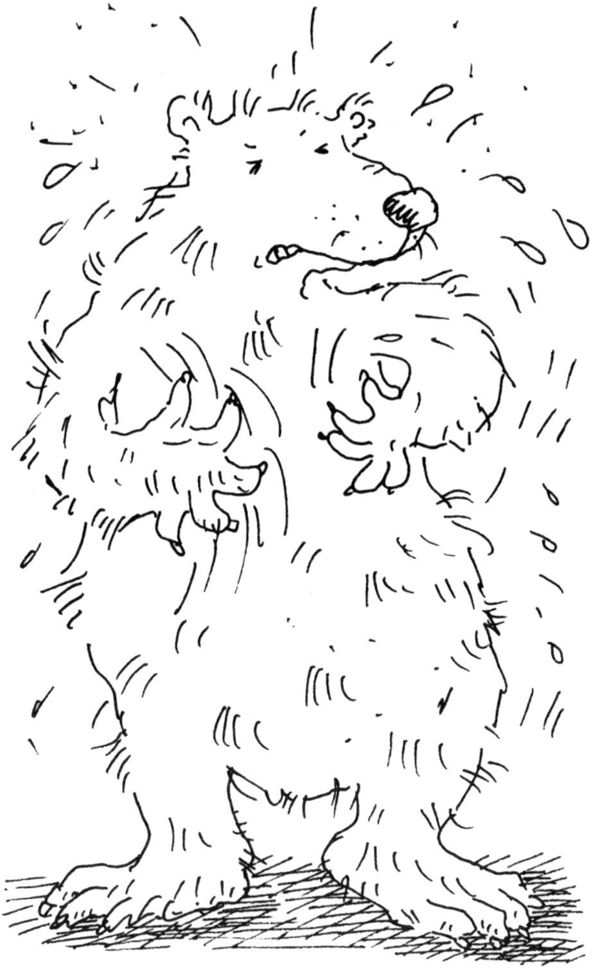

him. For a bear of his size he was very light on his paws. Rola Polar sat down and put his paws in the bowl. Then he gave a sigh of relief, muttering under his breath, 'Ah, ice cubes and igloos . . .'

'I could open the fridge door to keep you cool if you like,' Jamie said. They looked at each other.

'Better not,' said Rola Polar, 'remember what happened last time!' He gave his deep rumbling laugh and Jamie forgot to be worried and smiled. He remembered how they had gone off somewhere and left the fridge door open. When they got back there was water all over the floor and the food had turned a funny colour. There was a nasty smell too. Jamie's mother had been quite cross.

Rola Polar leant back and shut his eyes. Just for a moment he could imagine he was back home with the sound of water and tinkling ice.

He opened the zip pocket in his fur and took out two iced lollies and handed one to Jamie. They licked

them in silence until Jamie said in a
rush, 'I've got to pick up Mum's
shopping from Mr Bell at the
supermarket, but you needn't come.'
Jamie always spoke very fast when
he was worried about something.

'Oh, that's all right. Pleased to
lend you a paw,' said Rola Polar.
Jamie smiled happily.

12

When they were out on the street
some people noticed Rola Polar. But
quite often people just pushed past
and it was Rola Polar who was the
polite one, saying 'Excuse me', and
'I beg your pardon'. One old lady
ran into him with her basket on
wheels. 'Bears everywhere these
days,' she muttered crossly.

Rola Polar shifted the enormous striped umbrella which had WONDERFUL BUYS AT WATERFALL SUPERMARKETS on it. Jamie had found it at the back of a cupboard and it kept the sun off beautifully.

Inside the supermarket it was quite cool, which was a relief. But Mr Bell, who was an old friend, looked even more worried than Jamie.

'Oh what a dreadful morning,' he said. 'Something's gone wrong in the deep freeze room and the man hasn't been round to mend it yet. Your friend looks good holding our brolly. I hope everything doesn't melt. Oh dear, oh dear. I've put

your shopping in the usual place.
There's rather a lot, but perhaps
your friend will help you carry
it . . .'

Feeling quite important, Jamie led
the way.

'Ice caps and igloos,' he said as
they stepped inside the great cold
room stacked with food. Jamie made
straight for the shelf where he knew

16

his shopping would be. He didn't want to hang about. It was very cold even if the big deep freezes weren't working properly. And it was gloomy.

Rola Polar, on the other hand, felt instantly at home. He fluffed up his fur and stretched out his paws. He seemed to be getting sleeker by the minute.

'Wonderful,' he said dreamily.

'W-w-w-w . . .' said Jamie, but he couldn't get any further because his teeth were chattering too much. Rola Polar wandered round looking at everything and murmuring to himself until at last he noticed Jamie's pale face and chattering teeth.

'Time to go, but I'll just fix this first.'

And he unzipped his pocket, took out a small bag of tools and went over to the control panel where he turned and tightened and twisted. There was a whirr, the lights grew brighter and all the machines began to hum. The temperature dropped even further.

'It's all mended. My friend did it,' said Jamie to Mr Bell. 'He's very, very clever. He can mend anything in the whole world.' Rola Polar looked modestly at his back paws. Mr Bell was so pleased he gave Jamie a supermarket brolly and then presented them with an enormous chocolate iced cake.

'And if there's anything else you'd really fancy, just say the word,' he said, as he waved them off.

Once they had got home and stowed the food in the fridge, Jamie said sadly, 'I suppose you really ought to go home to the North Pole soon.'

'Nonsense,' said Rola Polar. 'There's still plenty to explore. What about a nice swim?'

'There isn't anywhere round here and the swimming pool's heated,' said Jamie. Rola Polar gave a shudder. The very idea of *warm* water made his fur stand up in tufts. 'But there is the old canal,' said Jamie, brightening.

Normally Jamie wouldn't have

gone near the canal because his
mother had told him not to go on his
own. Also the boys who teased him
went there to fish. But with Rola
Polar as his friend he wasn't alone.
And he wasn't afraid of anyone.

The water in the canal looked very
dirty and there were several rusty
old shopping trolleys in the water.
There was nobody about apart from
one man who was sitting on a stool
and holding a fishing rod in one
hand and a sandwich in the other.

'Bears everywhere these days,' he
muttered.

Rola Polar was much bigger and taller than Jamie, so he could see right over a big hedge of brambles and thistles.

'Let's explore the other side,' he said. 'One, two, three, *up*!'

Jamie climbed up on to his friend's shoulders and they went through the hedge as if it was made of grass.

'Igloos and ice caps,' they said together. The canal water on this side of the bramble hedge was clear, clean and cool-looking.

'Ah HA!' said Rola Polar as Jamie slid down, 'and very nice too. I think I'll just put a paw in . . .'

He behaved exactly like he did when they went to the play park. There he would whizz down the slide on one paw. Now he went head over heels, and stood on his front paws with his head under water.

He turned somersaults, paddled about on his back and then dived completely out of sight. When his nose finally bobbed up Jamie could see he was smiling from ear to ear. And suddenly Jamie felt very happy

too and he rolled up his jeans and
paddled.

If only they could stay here all the
time. Then Rola Polar might never
want to go back to the North Pole.
But what would Jamie's mother
say?

'There's something down here on the
bottom,' said Rola Polar, floating

past and looking rather like a furry
iceberg.

'Treasure?' asked Jamie hopefully.

'Ah . . .' said Rola Polar
mysteriously and vanished under the
water. He seemed to be gone a very
long time and Jamie was just
starting to get worried when he very,
very slowly reappeared, blowing out
a line of bubbles.

Rola Polar paused to get his breath back. His paws moved slowly under water like great paddles. 'Need all the help I can get,' he snorted.

Jamie waded in up to his waist, hands stretched out to grab at whatever it was that Rola Polar was towing up from the muddy bottom of the canal.

Jamie touched something cold and hard and slippery and then with a final push and pull and grunt IT came slowly out of the water.

Jamie sat down with a bump. IT was a bit of a let-down. It looked like one end of a very large, old and battered metal trunk. A sort of enormous box.

'Handsome, isn't it?' said Rola
Polar, getting his breath back and
wading ashore. 'Haven't seen one of
those for years. Now if we both pull
together . . .'

'Yes, but what *is* it?' asked Jamie
impatiently, when at last the 'thing'
was standing on the bank. Water
dripped slowly off its shabby sides.

'They used to call 'em ice boxes,'
Rola Polar replied. 'People had them
before there were refrigerators and
things. They kept big blocks of ice
in them and put their food on top.
How about a choc ice?'

'Yes, all right,' said Jamie,
'thanks. But what are we going to *do*
with it?'

Rola Polar smiled and leant back against the ice box. 'You'll see,' he said mysteriously.

Jamie's mother said several times how kind it was of Mr Bell to give them the chocolate cake. And Jamie nodded and mumbled and had another slice of toast. There was a lot to do and he quite wished his mother would go off to work.

'I can't think what you want all that old rope for,' she said. 'It used to be part of the drying rail I had in the kitchen before we got a proper spin dryer. You're too young to remember that. But I can't imagine *why* you want it!'

'Going fishing,' Jamie mumbled.

'You must be hoping to catch a
whale then!'

'Yes, sort of.'

Jamie's mother laughed all the
way to the bus stop, but to Jamie
and Rola Polar it was very serious
indeed.

'Splendid stuff,' said Rola Polar,
winding up the rope in a figure of

eight in a very neat way. They put up their supermarket brollies and went out into the bright, hot street. Rola Polar was so keen on his plan he just didn't notice the heat. They walked in step, with Rola Polar whistling and Jamie trying to copy him.

The fisherman was still by the canal with his mouth turned right down at the corners. He hadn't caught a single fish and Jamie wondered if he'd been there all night.

'Excuse me,' said Rola Polar in his most polite voice, 'my friend and I have come to tidy up some of the trolleys for the supermarket.'

'About time too,' said the fisherman.

Jamie and Rola Polar wheeled the
trolleys out of the water and up to
the hedge. Jamie climbed back up
on his friend's furry shoulders and
they were through.

The ice box had dried out nicely
and although still shabby it was no
longer dirty. But try as they might,
they could hardly shift it more than
a few inches. Jamie went scarlet and
Rola Polar went pale grey.

36

They rested for a few moments and then Rola Polar fetched the rope. They wound the rope round and round the box and tried to pull it through the hedge that way. They panted and puffed, but still it would not budge. Rola Polar and Jamie looked at each other in despair.

'Excuse me,' said a voice and they looked up. The fisherman was standing on a trolley, and looking down at them. 'That's a promising bit of water. Private is it?'

'No, rather not,' said Jamie firmly. 'We've just cleaned it up, but we can't shift this – er – box.'

'Very good for fishing, I expect,' said Rola Polar. 'And swimming,' he added with a sigh. Then Rola Polar saw how the fisherman could help. 'Perhaps if we passed the rope over to you and you pulled and we pushed . . .'

It was still hard work, but they managed it between the three of them. Luckily the box had made a

gap in the hedge just big enough for
the fisherman to get through without
catching his clothes on the brambles.

He now had a perfect way
through to the new bit of river. So he
was in a much better mood and
helped them rope the trolleys
together. Then they roped the ice
box on top.

'It's very nice having you bears about,' the fisherman said as the three of them shook hands. 'Now if you'll just excuse me – I've some fishing to do.' And he went off whistling to his own private pool.

Rola Polar took a pair of scissors out of his pocket and snipped off two more pieces of rope. Then he tied the brollies over the top of the laden trolleys.

It was lucky he was so large and strong because the trolleys just wouldn't go straight and squealed and squeaked from side to side. Some boys came running down the street and started to laugh and point, but Rola Polar gave them a LOOK and they went off without another word. Jamie could feel his whole face smiling.

'Ice cubes and igloos,' he and Rola Polar chanted together.

Mr Bell was just shutting up when he saw them coming.

'My goodness me, I haven't seen one of those old ice boxes since I was

your age, Jamie,' he said. 'We shall have to put you on the staff the way you've been advertising the supermarket all over the place. Everybody's looking at you. Now what can I do for you?'

Jamie and Rola Polar looked at each other. They were both thinking the same thing. Rola Polar gave a

great wink, and Jamie said to Mr
Bell, 'Please could we have some ice
cubes?'

'As many as you like,' said Mr Bell.

Mr Bell was as good as his word.
The ice rattled into the great trunk,
and the lid clanged shut. With Mr
Bell waving them off, Jamie and

Rola Polar made for the flats.

The lift only just took the ice box and the two of them, and creaked and groaned, but finally they made it to the roof.

It was very warm up there, but there was a faint breeze which ruffled Rola Polar's fur and cooled Jamie's scarlet face.

They tipped up the trolleys and slid the ice box into the shade of

46

Rola Polar's shed. Slowly he opened
up the lid and looked at all the ice
cubes. They had hardly melted at
all.

'Ahhhh,' said Rola Polar.

It was a great moment. Rola Polar
and Jamie shook hands. Then Rola
Polar lowered himself into the ice
with his head sticking out at one end
and his back paws at the other.

The breeze ruffled the two brollies. Rola Polar produced two extra special chocolate whirls from his pocket. The ice cubes rattled.

They looked at each other. This was even better than the North Pole because they could still be friends together. Then they both thought of the same thing at the same time.

'Ice cubes!' shouted Jamie.

'And igloos!' agreed Rola Polar patting his new home extension. They both laughed so much they had to have a lemon ice-cream whirl to recover . . .